TRAVELER'S HANDBOOK

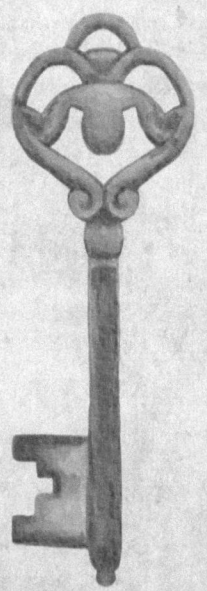

FOREWORD

Esteemed Traveler,

The art of Traveling is a revered and intricate skill, necessitating profound knowledge and diligent practice to safeguard all involved.

Engaging in Traveling without appropriate instruction may precipitate untold calamities, encompassing grievous injury and even death.

Therefore, it is imperative that all Travelers familiarize themselves with the entirety of this Handbook. Should you seek further elucidation, kindly consult your local Council of Elders.

INTRODUCTION

Welcome to the wondrous world of Travelers! As you hold this handbook in your hands, you are about to embark on a journey that will take you to places beyond your wildest imagination. This guide is designed to help you navigate the incredible adventures that await you as a keyholder. Whether you are a new Traveler just receiving your key on your 13th birthday or a seasoned explorer seeking deeper knowledge, this handbook is your essential companion.

Purpose of the Handbook

The purpose of "The Traveler's Handbook" is to provide you with the knowledge and tools you need to travel safely and responsibly. This manual is a comprehensive resource, containing everything from the basic functions of your key to advanced spells and the rules of The Academy. It is also a valuable reference for understanding the artifacts, creatures, and beings you may encounter on your journeys. Our goal is to ensure that you are well-prepared for the adventures ahead, whether you are exploring new worlds, traveling through time, or navigating the magical communities within our own world.

History of the Travelers and The Academy

The tradition of Traveling has been passed down through generations of keyholders, each one contributing to the rich tapestry of our history. The ability to Travel using a key is a rare and precious gift, one that comes with great responsibility. The Academy was established to help young Travelers like you learn how to use your abilities wisely and safely. Founded by the Ancestors, the Academy serves as a beacon of knowledge and a haven for those with the gift of traveling.

For centuries, the Academy has been the center of learning and exploration for keyholders. Here, you will not only learn how to use your key but also gain a deep understanding of the magical world and its many wonders. You will be guided by experienced faculty members, each with their unique expertise and knowledge, ensuring that you are well-equipped for your adventures.

Your Journey Begins

As you turn the pages of this handbook, you will discover the many aspects of being a Traveler. From mastering basic spells to understanding the rules that govern our community, from learning about the powerful artifacts to recognizing the various magical creatures you may encounter, this guide will be your trusted companion.

Remember, with great power comes great responsibility. Use your key wisely, respect the rules of The Academy, and always be mindful of the impact of your actions on the worlds you visit. The path of a Traveler is one of wonder, discovery, and endless possibilities. Embrace the journey, and may your travels be filled with adventure and enlightenment.

Welcome to the Travelers' community!

CHAPTER I
TRAVELING BASICS

The Key and Its Significance

Your key is more than just an object; it is the gateway to a world of endless possibilities. Each key is unique and bonded to its owner, a symbol of your status as a Traveler. When you received your key on your 13th birthday, you were entrusted with a powerful tool that can open doors to anywhere in the world, and for some, even to different times and dimensions.

How to Use Your Key

Simply hold it in your hand and focus your thoughts on the destination you wish to reach. Visualize the place clearly in your mind. Do not attempt to travel to an unknown location until you have mastered basic Traveling.

Once activated, a door will materialize and you can step through to your chosen destination.

Basic Traveler Etiquette

As a Traveler, you will encounter various cultures, beings, and environments. It is essential to conduct yourself with respect and consideration for the places and people you visit.

1. **Respect Local Customs:** Every place you visit may have its own customs and traditions. Take the time to learn and respect them.
2. **Do No Harm:** Avoid actions that could harm the environment, people, or creatures you encounter.
3. **Maintain Secrecy:** The existence of Travelers and the magical aspects of your journeys should be kept secret from non-Travelers to avoid unnecessary complications.

Safety Guidelines

Traveling can be exhilarating, but it also comes with risks. Follow these safety guidelines to ensure a safe and enjoyable experience:

1. **Travel with a Partner:** If possible, travel with a fellow keyholder. This provides an extra layer of safety and support.
2. **Stay Aware of Your Surroundings:** Be vigilant and aware of your environment at all times. Danger can come from unexpected places.
3. **Keep Your Key Secure:** Your key is your most valuable possession. Never leave it unattended or lend it to someone else.
4. **Know Your Limits:** Understand your abilities and do not push yourself beyond

what you can handle. It is okay to retreat and try again later.

5. **Emergency Procedures:** In case of an emergency, use the Call for Help spell (described in Chapter 2). This will alert nearby Travelers or Academy officials to your location.

By understanding and adhering to these essentials, you are well on your way to becoming a responsible and skilled Traveler. Your key is a powerful tool, and with it, you have the potential to explore and discover the wonders of the world. Use it wisely, and always remember the responsibilities that come with being a keyholder.

CHAPTER 2

TRAVELER'S CODE OF CONDUCT

As a Traveler, it is crucial to adhere to the rules and regulations that govern our community. These guidelines ensure the safety, respect, and harmony of all keyholders and the worlds they explore.

Traveler's Code of Conduct

All keyholders are expected to uphold the *Traveler's Code of Conduct*. These guidelines ensure that Travelers conduct themselves with integrity and respect while exploring different worlds and times.

1. Respect for Other Travelers

- **Collaboration:** Work together with fellow Travelers when possible. Share knowledge and experiences to enhance mutual understanding and safety.

- **Conflict Resolution:** Resolve conflicts peacefully and respectfully. Avoid actions that could harm or endanger other keyholders.

2. Use of Artifacts

- **Proper Handling:** Handle all artifacts with care and respect. Follow any specific guidelines provided for each artifact.
- **Ownership:** Respect the ownership of artifacts. Do not take or use artifacts that belong to others without permission.
- **Reporting Lost or Stolen Keys:** Immediately report any lost or stolen keys to Academy officials or the nearest Council of Elders. This ensures the security and proper tracking of all keys.

3. Maintaining Secrecy

- **Discretion:** Keep the existence of Travelers and the magical aspects of Traveling secret from non-Travelers. Revealing this information could lead to unwanted attention and complications.
- **Selective Sharing:** Only share information about Traveling with those who have been properly introduced and vetted by the Traveler community, such as non-Traveling spouses and some extended family members.

4. Responsibility to the Worlds Visited

- **Minimal Impact:** Leave no trace. Avoid actions that could alter or damage the environment, culture, or timeline of the worlds you visit.
- **Respect for Inhabitants:** Treat all inhabitants with kindness and respect. Understand and adhere to local customs and laws.

5. Personal Conduct

- **Ethical Behavior:** Conduct yourself ethically at all times. Avoid actions that could harm others or yourself.
- **Continuous Learning:** Commit to continuous learning and improvement. Seek knowledge and understanding to become a better Traveler.

Reporting and Accountability

If you witness any violations of these rules and guidelines, report them to the appropriate authorities within the Traveler community or the Academy. Accountability and transparency are essential to maintaining the integrity and safety of our community.

Summary

Adhering to the rules and regulations outlined in this chapter is essential for your success and safety as a Traveler. By following these guidelines, you contribute to the harmony and respect that define our community. Remember, being a keyholder is a privilege that comes with great responsibility. Use your abilities wisely and always strive to uphold the highest standards of conduct.

CHAPTER 3

TRAVELING TECHNIQUES

T raveling is the core skill that defines a Traveler. This chapter outlines the more advanced Traveling techniques, ensuring that you can navigate your journeys safely and effectively.

Advanced Traveling Techniques
Time Walking

Time Walking allows you to open a door leading to another time. It requires additional caution and precision and now requires a pre-authorized Time Travel Plan.

1. **Set the Time on the Watch:** Use the Time Watch to set the exact date and time you wish to travel to. Ensure the settings are accurate to avoid landing in an unintended era.
2. **Activate the Watch:** Take out your Key and focus on the specific time and date while holding the watch. The watch will glow,

indicating that you may open the door and cross over.

3. **Travel Safely:** Close the watch lid tightly so you don't inadvertently move the gears. Be mindful of the potential changes your presence might cause in the past or future.

4. **Going Home.** Simply take out your key and focus on home and the current date and year.

World Jumping

World Jumping allows you to travel to different worlds and dimensions. Only trained Travelers on Council missions may attempt World Jumping.

1. **Using the Sphere:** Take out your Key and Nuummite Sphere. When you door appears, you'll notice a dedicated socket to place your sphere. Once you place the Sphere, the door will disappear but the frame will remain. The space where the door used to be will be replaced by a portal. Use the Sphere in the socket as you would a trackball to scroll through destinations until you find the one you wish to visit. Pay attention to the color that glows in the socket. Red indicates an unsafe world, yellow indicates you should proceed with caution, and green indicates safe passage for human Travelers.

2. **Step Through:** Pocket the Sphere and step through the portal. Your location is tracked by the High Elf Council and, should you

need assistance, the Security Team can intervene.

3. **Report to local officials.** If the world is inhabited, immediately report to the governing body to announce your presence and request authorization.

Safety Tips for Advanced Traveling

1. **Avoid Your Own Timeline:** When time walking, avoid interacting with events that directly impact your own timeline to prevent paradoxes and confusion.
2. **Check Destination Safety:** Use the Sphere's guidance to ensure your destination is safe and stable before traveling.
3. **Maintain a Travel Log:** Keep a detailed log of your travels, including dates, times, and observations. This helps track your journeys and ensures you can replicate successful trips.

Emergency Procedures
Handling Emergencies

1. **Use the Call for Help Spell:** In case of an emergency, use the Call for Help spell to alert nearby Travelers or Academy officials of your location.
2. **Stay Calm:** Panic can exacerbate any situation. Stay calm and think clearly to assess your options.

3. **Return Immediately:** If you encounter danger, return to home immediately.
4. **Report Incidents:** Report any unusual or dangerous encounters to the Council for further investigation and support.

Summary

Traveling is a skill that requires practice, knowledge, and responsibility. By mastering both basic and advanced techniques and adhering to safety guidelines, you will become a proficient Traveler capable of exploring the world and beyond safely and effectively. Remember, every journey is an opportunity for learning and discovery. Travel wisely and with respect for the worlds you visit.

CHAPTER 4

THE ACADEMY

T he Academy serves as the central institution for educating and training young keyholders in the proper use of their abilities. This chapter provides an overview of The Academy's history, key figures, faculty, rules, and student life.

Overview of The Academy

The Academy is a prestigious institution designed to train and educate young Travelers, Time Walkers, and World Jumpers. The school is renowned for its rigorous curriculum, diverse faculty, and rich history. Students typically attend from age thirteen to eighteen, participating in summer programs and regular terms to master their skills and responsibilities. While the summer program is mandatory, attending college-level classes at The Academy after high school is only mandatory for Custodians. Tuition is free.

Campus Layout

The Academy is situated in a remote and magical location, accessible only through the use of keys by humans, and through portals by High-Elves. The dome-like location is referred to as a pocket world. The main building features a grand Main Hall with three large rooms opening off it, two on either side and one straight ahead, each with oversized French doors. The campus also includes dormitories, classrooms, dining facilities, and recreational areas.

Facilities

- **Main Hall:** The central hub for student activities and assemblies.
- **Dormitories:** Separate living quarters for boys and girls, with strict rules regarding curfews and inter-dorm visits.
- **Dining Room:** A large hall where meals are served, often themed to represent various cultures and cuisines.
- **Classrooms:** Specialized rooms equipped for teaching subjects like History, Latin, Magic,

Traveling, Martial Arts, Meditation, and Magical Communities.

- **Library:** A vast collection of books, including a special section for first editions and rare manuscripts.
- **Common Room:** A space for students to relax and socialize after meals and classes.
- **Faculty Living Quarters:** Faculty Members live on-site during the school year in a small mansion on the school grounds. To ensure their privacy, the building is cloaked and inaccessible to students.
- **Staff Living Quarters and other utility rooms as located in the basement.**

History and Founding

In the wake of the attacks on Witches and other magical beings, The Academy was established by the Ancestors to provide a safe place to offer structured education and training for keyholders. The goal was to ensure that young Travelers understood the responsibilities and potential of their abilities. The institution has grown over the centuries, adapting to new discoveries and challenges faced by the Traveler community.

Key Figures

Headmaster Lianon

Headmaster Lianon is a High Elf who oversees the administration of The Academy. Known for his wisdom and fair leadership, he ensures that both students and faculty uphold the school's standards.

Lady Samsara

Lady Samsara is a key member of the faculty, specializing in Traveling techniques and responsible for guiding students in mastering their key abilities. She is also involved in organizing field trips to other magical schools. She is in charge when Lianon is away.

Faculty

The Academy's faculty consists of a diverse group of beings, including humans, High Elves, Dwarves, and Fairies. This diversity enriches the learning experience, exposing students to various magical traditions and expertise.

- **Professor Elderberry:** Herbology teacher specializing in the healing arts.
- **Professor Brambles:** Instructor of Mindfulness and Meditation, focusing on mental discipline.
- **Professor Thunderbolt:** Instructor of Magic and Advanced Magic courses.
- **Doctor McClary:** Instructor of the History of Magic.
- **Sir Kravchuk:** Teaches Magical Communities, providing insights into the

different beings and societies students may encounter.

- **Master Smoke:** Martial Arts instructor, training students in physical combat and self-defense.

Academy Rules

The Academy serves as a training ground for young keyholders, providing the education and discipline necessary for responsible Traveling. The following rules are enforced to maintain order and safety within the Academy:

1. **Only registered students and authorized staff are permitted on campus.**
2. **Parents and visitors are welcome on Sundays from 1 to 4 p.m. and must arrive and depart from the Main Hall.** Visitors must sign in and out of the Register.
3. **Electronic devices will not function and are prohibited.**
4. **Alcohol, drugs, and tobacco are strictly prohibited on campus.**
5. **Students shall be in uniform at all times while on campus.** Casual attire is permitted within their respective dormitories.
6. **Students must attend all classes, meals, and assemblies that they are scheduled for.**
7. **Students shall maintain decorum and good behavior at all times.**

8. **Students must remain in their dormitories between 10 p.m. and 6 a.m.**
9. **Boys and girls must remain in their respective dormitories.**
10. **Students shall make every effort to achieve academic and personal success.**

Violations of these rules may result in disciplinary action, including temporary suspension of key privileges or expulsion from the Academy.

Student Life

Life at The Academy is structured yet dynamic, providing students with a balanced mix of academic rigor and extracurricular activities.

Daily Schedule

- **Morning Classes:** Typically run from 8 a.m. to 12 p.m., covering core subjects like History, Latin, and Magic.
- **Afternoon Classes:** From 1 p.m. to 3 p.m., focusing on practical skills like Martial Arts and Traveling techniques.
- **Evening Activities:** Students engage in various activities such as sports, meditation, and social events.

Summer Program

The Summer Program is an intensive training period where students from thirteen to eighteen years old learn about the Ancestors, key responsibilities, and advanced magical techniques. It includes a range of classes and activities designed to prepare students for their future roles as keyholders.

Extracurricular Activities

Students are encouraged to participate in extracurricular activities to broaden their skills and interests. These include sports, arts, and special interest clubs. The Academy also hosts social events, fostering a sense of community and camaraderie among students.

Summary

The Academy plays a vital role in shaping the future of the Traveler community. By providing comprehensive education and training, it ensures that young keyholders are well-prepared to navigate the complexities of their abilities and responsibilities. The diverse faculty, rigorous curriculum, and vibrant student life create an environment where students can thrive and grow into capable and responsible Travelers.

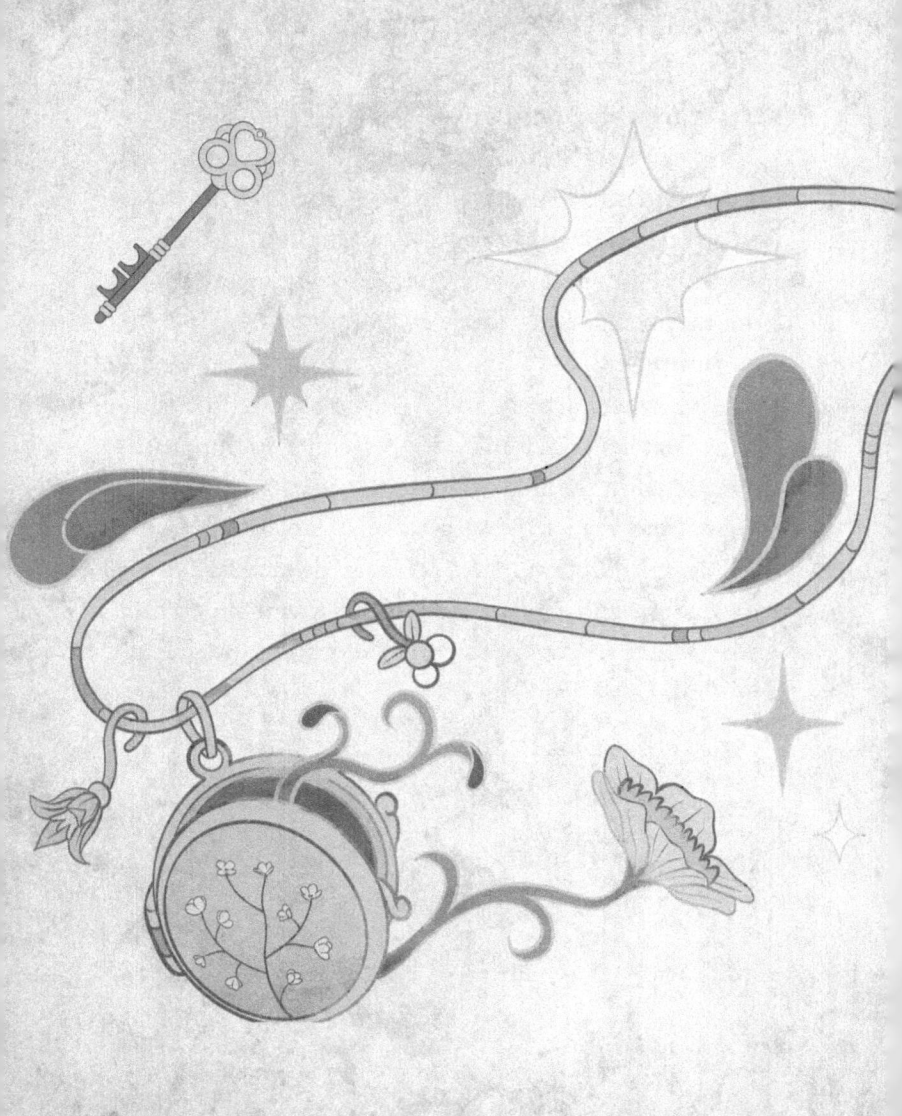

CHAPTER 5
SPELLS AND INCANTATIONS

As a Traveler, the ability to cast spells and perform incantations is a vital skill that will aid you in countless ways on your journeys. This chapter covers a range of spells from basic to advanced, ensuring that you are well-prepared for any situation you may encounter. Practice these spells regularly to master them and always use them responsibly.

Basic Spells

1. Creating a Window in a Traveling Door

Incantation: "Apertura Fenestrae"

This spell allows you to create a small, temporary window in a door created by your key. This is useful for peeking into your destination before fully entering.

Instructions: Hold your key to the center of the door and chant the incantation. A circular window will appear, allowing you to see through to the other side.

2. Creating a Light Orb

Incantation: "Lux Orbis"

This spell generates a small, glowing orb of light that

can float and follow you, providing illumination in dark places.

Instructions: Hold your hand out and visualize the light. Chant the incantation, and a glowing orb will form in your palm. Release it, and it will hover near you, lighting your path.

3. Fire-Starter Spell

Incantation: "Ignis Excito"

This spell ignites a small flame, useful for starting fires for warmth or cooking.

Instructions: Point your key at the desired location and chant the incantation. A small flame will appear where you direct it.

4. Invisibility Spell

Incantation: "Invisibilia"

This spell renders you invisible for a short period, allowing you to move unseen.

Instructions: Hold your key close to your heart, close your eyes, and chant the incantation. You will become invisible for approximately ten minutes.

5. Sound Bubble Spell

Incantation: "Sonus Bulla"

This spell creates a bubble of silence around you, blocking out external noise and preventing others from hearing you.

Instructions: Draw a circle in the air with your key and chant the incantation. A bubble will form around you, blocking out sound.

6. Calling a Drink of Water

Incantation: "Aqua Venire"

This spell summons fresh drinking water from the

air, providing hydration when needed.

Instructions: Hold your hand out and chant the incantation. Water will form in a small bubble in front of you, which you can drink from.

7. Shelter from the Rain Spell

Incantation: "Pluvia Defendo"

This spell creates a magical barrier that shields you from rain.

Instructions: Hold your key above your head and chant the incantation. A translucent dome will form, keeping you dry.

Advanced Spells

1. Duplication Spell

Incantation: "Duplicatio"

This spell creates a temporary duplicate of a small object.

Instructions: Hold the object in your hand and chant the incantation. A duplicate will appear beside it, lasting for up to an hour.

2. Time Rewind Spell (10 Seconds Back)

Incantation: "Tempus Reversus"

This spell allows you to rewind time by ten seconds, useful for correcting minor mistakes.

Instructions: Hold your key and visualize the moment you wish to rewind to. Chant the incantation, and time will reverse by ten seconds.

3. Protective Spells for Travelers

Incantation: "Protego Itineris"

This spell creates a protective barrier around you, shielding you from harm during your travels.

Instructions: Stand still and hold your key out in front

of you. Chant the incantation, and a shimmering barrier will form around you.

Tips for Spellcasting

1. **Practice Regularly:** Like any skill, spellcasting improves with practice. Dedicate time each day to practicing your spells.
2. **Stay Focused:** Concentration is key to successful spellcasting. Clear your mind of distractions before attempting a spell.
3. **Use Spells Wisely:** Remember that spells should be used responsibly. Avoid using them frivolously or in ways that could cause harm.
4. **Learn from Mistakes:** If a spell doesn't work as expected, take note of what went wrong and try again. Every mistake is an opportunity to learn.

By mastering these spells, you will be well-equipped to handle a variety of situations on your journeys. Use them wisely and always be mindful of the responsibilities that come with your abilities. Happy traveling!

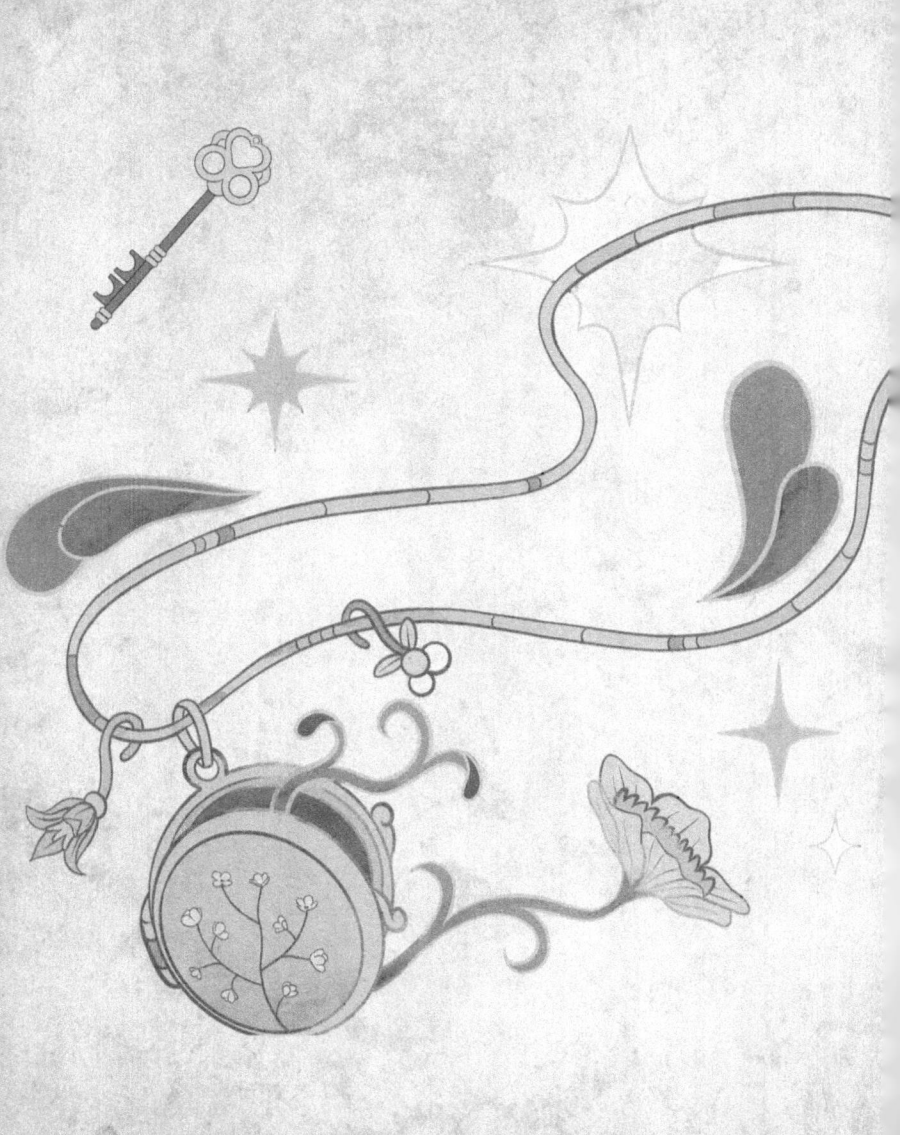

CHAPTER 6

MAGICAL ARTIFACTS

Artifacts are powerful objects imbued with magical properties that aid Travelers in their journeys. This chapter details some of the most significant artifacts mentioned in The Evers Series, their uses, and guidelines for handling them responsibly.

<u>The Time Watch</u>

The Time Watch is an antique pocket watch that allows its wearer to travel through time. It is intricately carved with the family motto and an hourglass design, symbolizing its connection to time.

How to Use the Time Watch

1. **Activating the Watch:** The watch has tiny gold arms and three rows of letters, numbers, and symbols that can be adjusted to set the time and date for travel.

2. **Traveling in Time:** By setting the desired time and date, and focusing on the destination, the Traveler can move through time.

Historical Context

The Time Watch was found in Simon's room and is believed to have been used by their father for time travel.

<u>The Sphere (Nuummite Sphere)</u>

The Sphere, often mistakenly referred to as a marble, is crafted from Nuummite, also known as the Sorcerer's Stone. This ancient stone is capable of storing unlimited amounts of information and is used for world jumping.

How to Use the Sphere

1. **Setting the Destination:** Communicate the desired destination to the Sphere verbally or telepathically while holding it.
2. **Activating the Sphere:** Place the Sphere in the door socket to input the coordinates of the destination and the return location. The Sphere will glow when ready.
3. **Traveling Safely:** The Sphere will suggest safe locations based on the Traveler's requirements, ensuring only secure destinations are chosen .

Origins

The High Elves gifted each of the original twelve

Elders with a Nuummite Sphere to study other worlds and gather knowledge. These Spheres are interconnected, sharing collective knowledge of all voyages.

The Archivum

The Archivum is a vast repository of knowledge, containing records of all known worlds, creatures, and magical phenomena. It is an essential resource for Travelers seeking information on their journeys.

How to Access the Archivum

1. **Using the Key:** Insert your key into the lock on the Archivum's door. The door will open to reveal the library.
2. **Searching for Information:** Use the index to locate the desired records. The Archivum's magical catalog will guide you to the appropriate section.
3. **Recording New Information:** Record new information in a journal and place it in the designated area for updates. The Archivum will incorporate it into the main collection.

Handling and Care of Artifacts

1. **Proper Storage:** Keep artifacts in a secure and safe place when not in use. Many artifacts are sensitive to environmental conditions and should be stored accordingly.

2. **Regular Maintenance:** Some artifacts require regular maintenance to function correctly. Follow the specific guidelines for each artifact.

3. **Respect Ownership:** Artifacts are often passed down through families or entrusted to specific individuals. Respect the ownership and use of artifacts responsibly.

Summary

Artifacts are powerful tools that greatly enhance a Traveler's abilities. Understanding their uses and handling them with care is essential for success and safety. Always follow the provided guidelines and seek further instruction from experienced Travelers or Academy officials if needed.

CHAPTER 7
MAGICAL BEINGS AND CREATURES

In the world of Travelers, encounters with various magical creatures and beings are inevitable. Understanding these beings, their characteristics, and how to interact with them is crucial for a Traveler. This chapter provides an overview of some of the most notable magical creatures and beings you may encounter.

High Elves

Description and Habitat

High Elves are tall, elegant beings known for their wisdom, magical abilities, and longevity. They typically grow to seven feet tall, with some Ancient Elves reaching up to nine feet. High Elves have fair porcelain skin and long silver-blond hair. They reside in the Summer Isles, a place of extraordinary beauty and magic, where they live in communities based on occupation and family status.

Interaction Guidelines

1. **Respect:** Always show respect when interacting with High Elves. They value courtesy and politeness.
2. **Telepathy:** Many High Elves can communicate telepathically. Be mindful of your thoughts, as they may be able to perceive them.
3. **Cultural Norms:** Familiarize yourself with their customs, such as waiting to be invited to speak and showing deference to elders and council members.

Dwarves

Description and Habitat

Dwarves are stout, strong beings known for their craftsmanship and resilience. They are shorter than humans, with a stocky build and a predisposition for manual labor and engineering. Dwarves are often found living in mountainous regions or underground communities.

Interaction Guidelines

1. **Pride:** Dwarves are very proud beings. Compliment their work and show appreciation for their craftsmanship.
2. **Temperament:** They can be quick to anger and hold grudges, so tread carefully in conversations.
3. **Etiquette:** Address them formally and avoid making assumptions about their abilities or limitations.

Goblins

Description and Habitat

Goblins are smaller than humans, with distinctive features such as hooked noses and long pointy ears. They are resourceful and often involved in trading and crafting.

Interaction Guidelines

1. **Curiosity:** Goblins are naturally curious but may find staring uncomfortable. Be mindful of your behavior when meeting them for the first time.
2. **Respect:** Show respect for their culture and practices. They appreciate directness and honesty.
3. **Trade:** When trading with Goblins, ensure you understand the value of what you are exchanging to avoid misunderstandings.

Other Magical Beings

General Characteristics and Abilities

- **Elves:** There are various types of Elves, including the shorter Keebler-like Elves and the majestic High Elves. They are known for their agility, magical abilities, and connection to nature.
- **Fairies and Pixies:** Small, winged beings known for their playful nature and magical dust that can enchant objects or beings.
- **Mermaids and Sirens:** Aquatic beings with the upper body of a human and the lower body of a fish. They are known for their enchanting voices.
- **Valkyries:** Warrior maidens who serve the gods and are known for their strength and combat skills.

Interaction Guidelines

1. **Understand Differences:** Each species has its unique customs and abilities. Take the time to learn about them before interacting.
2. **Respect Boundaries:** Be aware of and respect the personal space and cultural boundaries of each being.
3. **Communication:** Many magical beings have their own languages and ways of communication. Learning a few basic phrases can go a long way in building rapport.

Summary

Understanding the diverse array of magical creatures and beings you may encounter as a Traveler is essential for your safety and success. By respecting their customs, showing courtesy, and being mindful of their abilities and characteristics, you will be well-equipped to navigate your interactions with these extraordinary beings.

CHAPTER 8
THE HIGH ELVES

The High Elves, also known as the Altmer, are one of the most ancient and powerful races in the magical world. They reside primarily on the Summer Isles, a place of extraordinary beauty and advanced magical technology. This chapter delves into their powers, living arrangements, the unique environment of the Summer Isles, and the work they do there.

High Elves (Altmer)
Powers and Abilities

High Elves are known for their significant magical abilities and longevity. They possess natural proficiency in various magical disciplines, including telepathy, healing, and elemental magic. Their inherent magical prowess is complemented by centuries of study and practice.

1. **Telepathy:** Many High Elves can communicate telepathically, a skill that allows

for silent, instant communication over distances.
2. **Healing:** They possess advanced healing abilities, capable of curing wounds and illnesses that are beyond the capabilities of human medicine.
3. **Elemental Magic:** High Elves can manipulate the elements, using their powers to control fire, water, earth, and air for various purposes.

Ancient High Elves

Ancient High Elves are the oldest and most revered members of their race, often reaching heights of up to nine feet. They possess immense wisdom and magical power, having lived through many ages and witnessed significant historical events.

Role in Society

1. **Mentorship:** Ancient High Elves often serve as mentors and advisors to younger Elves, sharing their vast knowledge and experience.
2. **Council Leadership:** Many Ancient High Elves hold positions on the Council, guiding the community with their deep understanding of history and magic.
3. **Guardians of Knowledge:** They are responsible for maintaining and expanding the Archivum, ensuring that valuable knowledge is preserved for future generations.

The Summer Iles

The Summer Isles are the homeland of the High Elves. Located on the planet Nurn, it is a place of unparalleled beauty and magical energy. The islands are accessible by boat within the planet, or by Elven Portal.

Environment and Technology

The Summer Isles boast lush greenery, pristine bodies of water, and an unmarred sky. The island's environment is maintained through a combination of natural processes and advanced magical techniques.

1. **Natural Growth:** The island's flora thrives without rain, drawing water directly from the soil. The air is infused with a natural ozone-like freshness, making the environment exceptionally pleasant.

2. **Magical Technology:** High Elves use advanced magical technology in their daily lives. For example, their homes are equipped with devices similar to tablets that control various functions through touch and intent.

3. **Sustainability:** The Elves live in harmony with nature, using their magic to support and enhance the natural environment rather than exploit it. This results in a sustainable lifestyle that leaves minimal impact on the ecosystem.

Council and Governance

The High Elves are governed by a Council that includes representatives from each of the main occupations: knowledge, science, food production, wellness, land maintenance, and engineering. The Council ensures that decisions benefit the entire community and maintains the island's well-being.

Knowledge Sharing

The High Elves have developed several sophisticated methods to share and acquire knowledge, leveraging their advanced magical abilities and technology to ensure efficient communication and education.

1. **Telepathic Communication:** High Elves commonly use telepathy for instant and secure communication, allowing them to share thoughts and information without the need for physical devices.
2. **Magical Tablets:** They use devices similar to tablets that store and display vast amounts of information. These tablets are operated through touch and intent, making them intuitive and easy to use.

3. **Knowledge Cubes:** Knowledge cubes are a unique method of information transfer among the High Elves. These cubes can store and transmit knowledge directly to an individual through touch. The knowledge is indexed and divided into manageable parcels tailored to the recipient's capacities and area of interest. This method allows for the transfer of both theoretical knowledge and experiential learning.

4. **The Archivum:** The Archivum is a vast repository maintained by the Council of Earthly Magical Beings. It contains extensive records on all known worlds, magical creatures, and phenomena, serving as a comprehensive reference for both educational and research purposes. The Archivum is continuously updated and is accessible through magical means.

5. **Traditional Learning:** Despite their advanced methods, High Elves also value traditional learning through reading texts and attending lectures. This method remains important for transmitting complex and detailed information that benefits from in-depth study and discussion.

Key Facilities on the Summer Isles

The Summer Isles are equipped with various facilities that reflect the High Elves' commitment to knowledge, well-being, and innovation.

1. **The Knowledge Center:** This central hub is where High Elves gather to study, share information, and conduct research. It includes classrooms, meeting rooms, and areas for using knowledge cubes. The center also hosts lectures from Ancient Elves and visiting scholars from other worlds.

2. **The Wellness Center:** Similar to the best spas on Earth, the Wellness Center offers a range of treatments using natural resources from the island, such as mineral water from caves and mud from waterfalls. It is designed to promote relaxation and well-being among the High Elves.

3. **The Science Center:** A place dedicated to innovation and research, the Science Center allows High Elves to explore and develop new technologies and magical techniques. It includes laboratories and facilities for conducting experiments and testing new ideas.

Lifestyle and Living Arrangements

High Elves live in well-organized communities that reflect their values of harmony, efficiency, and respect for nature. Their living arrangements are designed to foster a sense of community while accommodating the varying needs of individuals and families.

1. **Family Communities:** High Elves who choose to have families live in spacious homes

within communities designed for families. These areas include playgrounds and schools, creating a supportive environment for raising children.

2. **Single Communities:** Elves who do not choose mates live in shared dwellings with others in similar situations. These communities are often organized by occupation, facilitating collaboration and shared interests.

3. **Couple Communities:** Pairs of High Elves who do not have children live in smaller dwellings suited for two. These communities are randomly placed to encourage diversity and interaction among different groups.

4. **Sustainability and Harmony:** The High Elves live in harmony with nature, using their magic to enhance the environment rather than exploit it. This results in a sustainable lifestyle with minimal impact on the ecosystem.

Summary

The High Elves are a powerful, wise, and harmonious race, living in a land that reflects their values and abilities. Their advanced magical skills, sustainable living practices, and collaborative communities set an example for other magical beings. Understanding the High Elves and their way of life provides valuable insights into the broader magical world and the potential for harmony between nature and magic.

COUNCILS OF THE MAGICAL WORLD

I n the intricate and interconnected world of magic, councils play a pivotal role in maintaining order, governance, and the dissemination of knowledge. Three of the most significant councils are the Council of Elders, the Council of Earthly Magical Beings, and the High Elf Council. This chapter explores the roles, functions, and significance of these councils.

Council of Elders

The Council of Elders is composed of experienced Custodians who oversee the responsibilities and training of keyholders. The term "Elder" refers to the head of a family, regardless of age.

1. **Custodian Guidance:** Elders provide guidance and mentorship to new Custodians, ensuring they understand their duties and responsibilities.

2. **Knowledge Preservation:** The Council of Elders plays a crucial role in preserving the knowledge and traditions of the Travelers. They contributed to creating the Archivum, a comprehensive book of knowledge and spells.

3. **Conflict Resolution:** When disputes arise among Custodians, the Council of Elders mediates and resolves conflicts to maintain harmony within the community.

Access and Membership

Members of the Council of Elders are typically chosen based on their experience and contributions to the Traveler community. They serve as long-term custodians of knowledge and traditions.

Council of Earthly Magical Beings

The Council of Earthly Magical Beings oversees the collective Councils of Elders for Travelers. It acts as the governing body for all magical beings on Earth, ensuring coordination and cooperation among various magical communities.

1. **Governance and Regulation:** This council governs the activities of magical beings on Earth, creating laws and regulations to maintain order and prevent misuse of magical powers.

2. **Education and Training:** The council is responsible for establishing educational

institutions like The Academy, where young Travelers and magical beings can learn about their heritage and develop their skills.

3. **Sanctioning and Justice:** It adjudicates cases involving misuse of magic or breaches of magical laws, ensuring justice is served and the safety of both the magical and Traveler communities is upheld.

Access and Membership

Members of the Council of Earthly Magical Beings are drawn from various magical races and communities. They are selected based on their expertise, integrity, and contributions to the magical world.

High Elf Council

The High Elf Council is the governing body of the High Elves, one of the most ancient and powerful races in the magical world. This council oversees the welfare, governance, and development of the High Elf community, particularly on the Summer Isles.

1. **Community Governance:**
2. The High Elf Council governs the day-to-day activities and long-term planning of the High Elf community, ensuring harmony and progress.
3. **Knowledge and Research:**
4. This council is heavily involved in preserving and expanding the knowledge of the High

Elves. It oversees the Archivum and other repositories of knowledge, ensuring they are up-to-date and accessible.

5. **Inter-Species Relations:**

6. The High Elf Council maintains relations with other magical races and human societies, ensuring cooperation and mutual respect. They also play a role in educating other magical beings and humans about High Elf culture and knowledge.

Access and Membership

The High Elf Council includes representatives from each main occupation within the High Elf community, such as knowledge, science, food production, wellness, land maintenance, and engineering. Council members are elected by the community and serve terms of one hundred years.

Summary

The Councils of the magical world are integral to maintaining order, governance, and the dissemination of knowledge among magical beings and Travelers. Each council plays a specific role in overseeing their respective communities, ensuring that the traditions and responsibilities are upheld, and that justice and harmony are maintained. Understanding the functions and significance of these councils provides valuable insights into the structure and governance of the magical world.

GLOSSARY OF TERMS

Understanding the terminology used in the world of Travelers is crucial for new keyholders. This glossary provides definitions for key concepts, items, spells, and other terms you may encounter in your journeys.

A

Archives: A rare and valuable book of spells dating back to the beginning of Travelers. It is said to have been gifted to humans with the keys by the Ancestors.

Artifacts: Magical objects imbued with special powers, used by Travelers for various purposes. Examples include the Time Watch and the Nuummite Sphere.

B

Basic Spells: Fundamental spells that every Traveler learns, such as creating a light orb, starting a fire, and turning invisible for a few seconds.

Beings: Various magical creatures and entities that Travelers may encounter. Examples include High Elves, Dwarves, and Goblins.

C

Custodian: A designated individual responsible for safeguarding the keys and the Archives. Custodians have the authority to revoke keys if necessary.

Council of Earthly Magical Beings: A Council comprised of Travelers, Witches and other magical beings living on Earth.

Council of Elders: A governing body that oversees the conduct of Travelers and handles serious matters such as key revocations and rule enforcement.

D

Dwarves: Stout, strong beings known for their craftsmanship and resilience. They are proud and quick to anger, often living in mountainous regions or underground communities.

E

Elder: Head of a Family. What a Custodian becomes after he trains his replacement and they take over as Custodian.

Evers: A family of keyholders with a long history of Traveling. The Evers family holds multiple keys and has significant responsibilities within the Traveler community.

F

Fairies: Small, winged beings known for their playful nature and magical dust that can enchant objects or beings.

G

Goblins: Smaller than humans, Goblins have distinctive features such as hooked noses and long pointy ears. They are resourceful and often involved in trading and crafting.

H

High Elves: Tall, elegant beings known for their wisdom, magical abilities, and longevity. They reside at The Summer Isles and are highly respected within the magical community.

Hold (The): A magical prison under the direction of the Council for Earthly Magical Beings

I

Invisibility Spell: A spell that renders the caster invisible for a short period, typically around fifteen seconds.

J

Jumping (World Jumping): The act of traveling between different worlds or dimensions using a Nuummite Sphere. This requires setting coordinates and using a special control panel.

K

Key: A magical object that allows its holder to open portals to different locations and times. Each key is unique and bonded to its owner.

Keyless Travelers: Individuals who have had their keys revoked but still retain the ability to travel with the help of another keyholder.

M

MFO: Magical Foreign Office.

Multiverse – The collection of parallel and pocket worlds. Not to be confused with the human concept of multiverse.

N

Nuummite Sphere: An artifact used for World Jumping. It can store vast amounts of information and provide safe travel destinations for the user.

P

Portal – A Magical window used by High Elves and World Jumpers to travel anywhere.

Protective Spells: Spells designed to protect Travelers from harm during their journeys. Examples include creating a shield or barrier.

R

Repository: A secure and sacred place where the keys of all keyholders, especially those who are no longer active Travelers or have passed on.

Revoking Incantation: A spell used by Custodians to revoke a key from a Traveler who has misused it.

S

Seelie Court - Fairies that are said to be human-friendly, warning them when they are in danger, asking for help when they cannot accomplish a task, and are generally thought to be happy and benign.

Sound Bubble Spell: A spell that creates a bubble of silence around the caster, blocking out external noise and preventing others from hearing them.

Summer Isles – Magical dwelling place of the High Elves.

T

Time Watch: An artifact that allows its wearer to travel through time by setting the desired date and time. It is an essential tool for Time Travelers.

Traveling: The act of moving between different locations, times, or dimensions using a key or other magical artifacts.

Traveling Letter: A note or letter folded in such a way. It can cross time and space and will always reach its destination.

TTP: Time Travel Plan, a plan that must be approved before embarking on a time journey.

U

Unseelie – Fairies that are said to be the unholy fairies, those that seek to harm humans, the ones that steal babies and the like.

V

Vault (Teleportation Vault): A secure storage device that can transport items to and from different locations, often used for sending supplies or important documents.

W

World Jumper: A Traveler who uses the Nuummite Sphere to travel between different worlds. World Jumpers are rare and often have specialized training.

FREQUENTLY ASKED QUESTIONS

Frequently Asked Questions (FAQs)

As a new Traveler, you are bound to have many questions about your key, traveling techniques, and the magical world. This chapter addresses some of the most frequently asked questions to help you navigate your journey more confidently.

General Questions

Q1: What is the primary function of a key?

A: The key is a magical object that allows its holder to open doors to different locations and times. Each key is unique and bonded to its owner. It is the primary tool for all Travelers.

Q2: How do I activate my key?

A: Hold the key in your hand, focus on the desired destination, and visualize it clearly in your mind. The key will start to warm up and glow, indicating it is ready, and a door will appear.

Q3: Can I travel anywhere with my key?

A: While the key allows you to travel to many places, it is essential to ensure that your destination is safe and suitable. Some locations may have restrictions or require additional preparations.

Safety and Security

Q4: What should I do if I lose my key?

A: Report the loss immediately to your Custodian, local Council or Academy official. Lost keys are typically returned to the family's Repository within twenty-four hours.

Q5: How can I ensure my safety while traveling?

A: Always travel with a partner if possible, be aware of your surroundings, and keep your key secure. Plan your return journey in advance to avoid being stranded. Familiarize yourself with the basic and advanced spells to aid you in case of emergencies.

Q6: What should I do in case of an emergency?

A: Use the Call for Help spell to alert nearby Travelers or Academy officials. Stay calm, assess the situation, and return to a safe location immediately. If necessary, contact the Academy for further assistance.

Traveling Techniques

Q7: How do I travel through time using the Time Watch?

A: Set the exact date and time on the Time Watch and focus on your destination. The watch will glow when it is ready for time travel. Open your door and step through.

Q8: What is world jumping, and how do I do it?

A: World jumping is the act of traveling between different worlds or dimensions using a Nuummite Sphere. Hold the Sphere, focus on your desired destination, and set the coordinates using the door socket. The Sphere will glow when it is ready for travel. Step through the door with confidence, knowing the Sphere has guided you to a safe location.

Q9: Can I visit any world with the Nuummite Sphere?

A: The Nuummite Sphere will suggest safe locations based on your requirements. It is essential to follow these suggestions to ensure your safety and avoid dangerous or unstable worlds. Only High Elvers can visit all worlds.

Rules and Regulations

Q10: What happens if I break the rules outlined in the Traveler's Handbook?

A: Breaking the rules can result in disciplinary actions, including the revocation of your key. If the key is revoked by a Custodian, it may be returned upon review. However, if the key is revoked magically, you become a keyless Traveler and must travel with another keyholder.

Q11: Are there any restrictions on who I can travel with?

A: While there are no specific restrictions on travel companions, it is essential to ensure that they understand and respect the rules of traveling. Traveling with another keyholder is recommended for safety and support.

Q12: How do I report misuse of a key?

A: If you witness or suspect misuse of a key, submit a complaint to the Council of Elders. Underage Travelers may also submit a complaint to the Headmaster for matters requiring discretion.

Miscellaneous

Q13: What should I do if I encounter a magical creature or being?

A: Treat all magical creatures and beings with respect and courtesy. Familiarize yourself with their customs and abilities before interacting. If you are unsure, consult the Archivum or a knowledgeable faculty member at the Academy.

Q14: How can I improve my traveling skills?

A: Practice regularly, stay focused, and continuously seek knowledge and guidance from experienced Travelers and faculty members. Participate in Academy programs and extracurricular activities to enhance your skills.

Q15: Is there a support network for Travelers?

A: Yes, the Traveler community is a close-knit network that provides support and assistance to its members. Reach out to fellow Travelers, Academy officials, or your country's Council of Elders for help and guidance whenever needed.

About the Author

Marie-Helene Lebeault lives in Quebec, Canada and is the mother of two young adults. A retired teacher, she now spends her days writing, translating academic manuals, and lending her voice to corporate training videos. She enjoys reading, hiking, and going to the beach.

Follow her on Social Media, she'd love to hear from you!

To join her newsletter, visit her website at www. mhlebeault.com

- facebook.com/mhlebeaultauthor
- x.com/mhlebeault
- instagram.com/mhlebeault
- amazon.com/author/mhlebeault
- bookbub.com/authors/marie-helene-lebeault
- goodreads.com/mhlebeault
- linkedin.com/in/mhlebeault
- tiktok.com/@mhlebeaultauthor
- youtube.com/@mhlebeault

Also by the Author

The Chronicles of the Starborne Cadets

Stars Beyond Realms

Shadows of Orion

Echoes of the Void

The Nebula's Heart

The Starborne Paradox

Defenders of the Realm

A Journey to Power

The Quest for the Emerald Rattleback

A Summer of Discovery

The Quest for the Sacred Tree

A Summer of Opposites

The Quest for the Phantom Feather

A Summer of Courage

The Quest for the Kraken's Ink

A Summer of Destiny

The Quest for the Cursed Mirrors

The Evers Series

The Ancestors' Key

The Academy

The Time Walker

The World Jumper

Blood Magick Trilogy

The Blood Mage

Blood Magick

Blood Legacy

Standalones

Clarity Castle

What Happens Next?

Ghost Stories

Holiday Shifters

Echoes of Tomorrow

Utopia

Picture Books

Fairy Grandmother: Millie Goes to Antarctica

Fairy Grandmother: Millie Goes to the North Pole

Fairy Grandmother: Millie Goes to China

Fairy Grandmother: Millie Goes to Africa

(Also available in French, Spanish, German, and Italian)

www.ingramcontent.com/pod-product-compliance
Lightning Source LLC
Chambersburg PA
CBHW020332130626
46549CB00003B/1143